HIPHOP_AND_
FRIENDS

Scan this nametag on Instagram to follow
hiphop_and_friends.

HIP HOP & FRIENDS

Written and Illustrated by
Lawrence Engerman Jr.

I Can!
I Can't!

BLUES
the
BEE

HIP HOP
the
RABBIT

RHYTHM
the RAT

Typeset in Adobe Indesign.
Illustrations rendered with PITT Artist Pens, Elite
Colored Pencils and Markers.

Book logo Design by Precision Printing.

Published and Distributed by Urban Nation Entertainment.
904 W. Montgomery Ste. 4-326
Willis, TX
77378

To Elia and Emyah
My Beautiful Girls

Jump, jump let me see!
I will count.
I will count to three.

No, I will not jump!
I can't jump.
Just let me be.

You can count all you want,
but I still won't jump in three.

You could if you would.
I know you just don't.

I can't if I could.
You would but I won't.

Then run, run!
Let me see that!

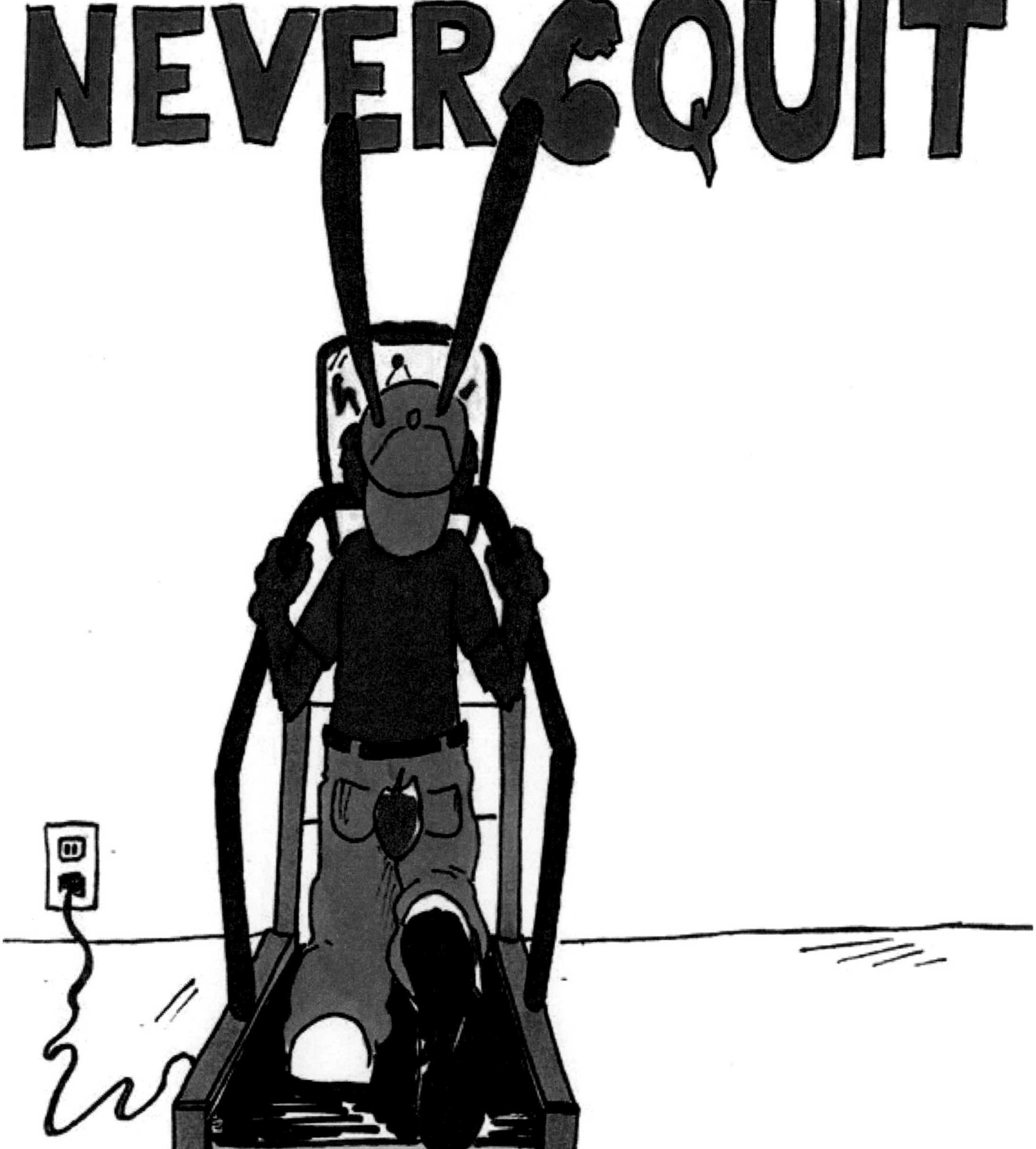
NEVER QUIT

You won't see me run.
I can't run in fact.

I won't run!
I can't run!
I can't run at all!

You could, but I can't.

See, I just might fall!

Well, I can do anything!
I know that
I could!

13

Well, I can't do anything!
Is that understood?

I can't run
or jump
or anything else.

Because "I can't; I can't,"
is what you tell yourself.

**Just say you could,
just one time,**

YOU CAN

and watch what you
can do when you've
changed your mind.

DO IT!

I will not and
cannot change
my mind.

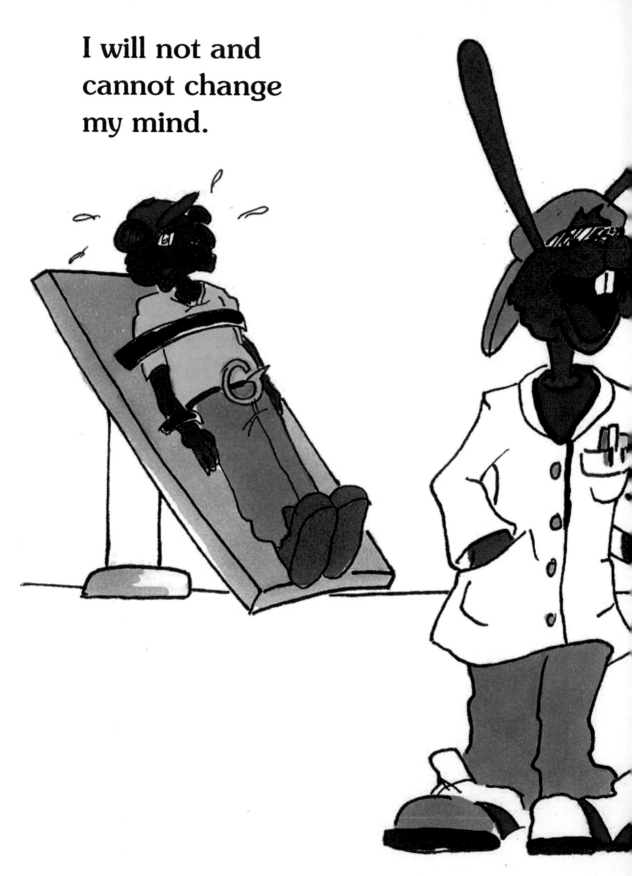

Why would I do that and waste my time?

I'm

Only haste is waste
or to not even try.

Why do nothing at all
and watch time fly by?

Just, because.

Just, because what?

I don't know.

Maybe I'm not too tough.

You don't need to be tough.
You just need to believe.

SUPER

You'll be amazed by
what you can achieve!

Alright then,
I'll give it a shot.

I'll try to jump
and run up
the block.

**If I don't make it,
then I'll have to stop.**

I will have to quit
before I drop.

Just believe
you'll reach the top.

Please don't stop!

Keep on going
and going!

Keep on knowing
that you
could.

Keep on showing
that you would
make it if you tried.

Never give up.

Dig deep inside.

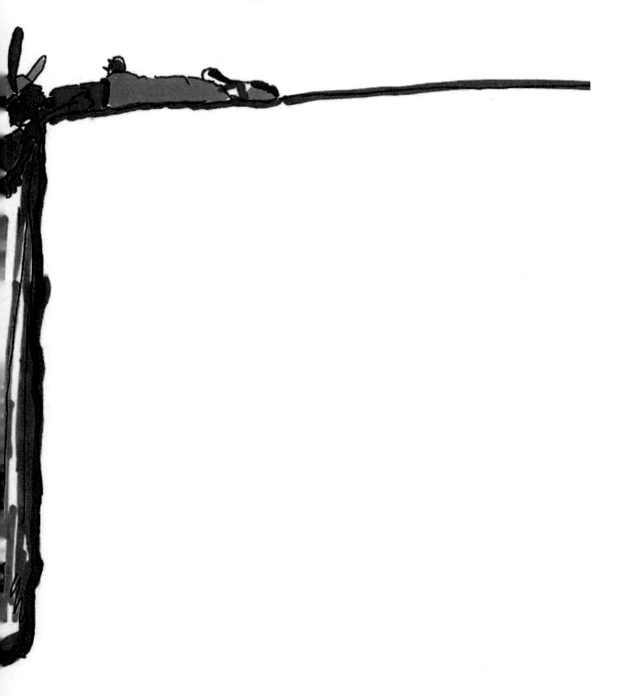

Watch when your mind
and heart collide.

Great things happen
when you believe in "I."

I believe now.
I know that
I can!

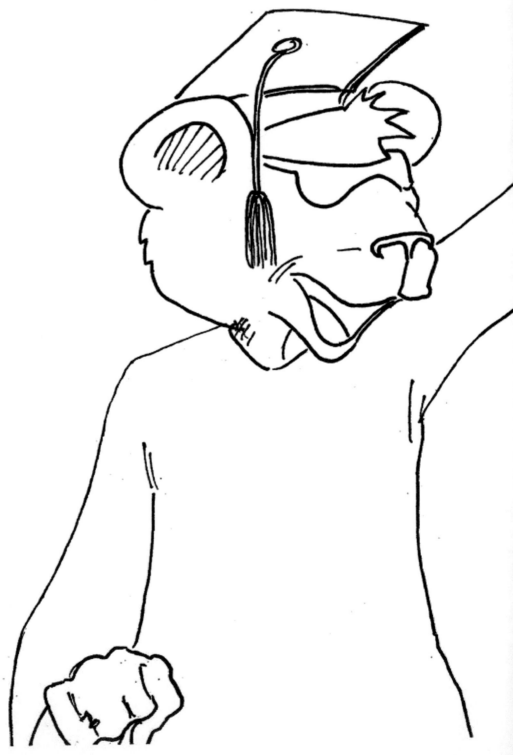

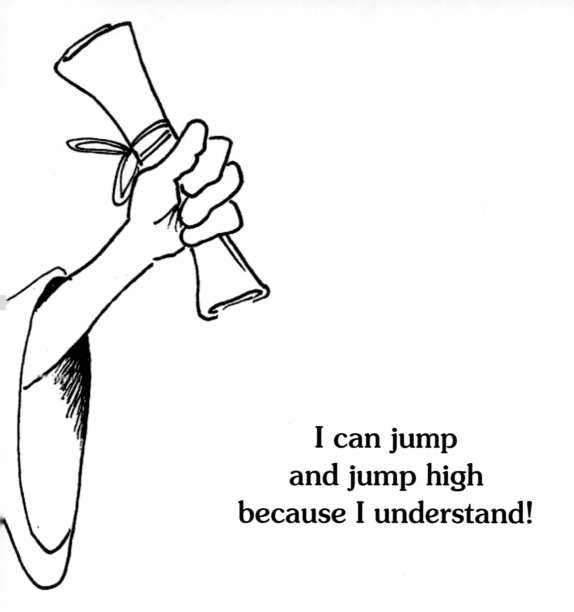

**I can jump
and jump high
because I understand!**

I will reach the top!
I will not stop
until I'm through!

It is I who makes
the difference
in everything
I do!

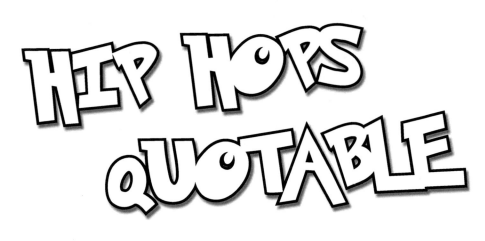

HIP HOPS QUOTABLE

The moral of the story is believe in you,

and all the great things that you can do.

Never say you can't, only that you could.

Give it all you have, and watch you feel good.

It never hurts to try, only if you don't.

So always say you would, never that you won't.

Say I can do it.

I know I can do it.

I can do anything

When I put my mind to it.

I can do anything

When I put my mind to it.

Made in the USA
San Bernardino, CA
19 July 2019